Creepy Creatures

Caterpillars

Sarah Chappelow

Raintree

Chicago, Illinois

© 2006 Raintree
Published by Raintree, a division of Reed Elsevier, Inc.
Chicago, Illinois
Customer Service 888-363-4266
Visit our website at www.raintreelibrary.com

Printed and bound by South China Printing Company.
10 09 08 07 06
10 9 8 7 6 5 4 3 2 1

Library of Congress Cataloging-in-Publication Data:
Chappelow, Sarah.
   Caterpillars / Sarah Chappelow.
      p. cm. -- (Creepy creatures)
   Includes index.
   ISBN 1-4109-1767-3 (library binding - hardcover) -- ISBN 1-4109-1772-X (pbk.)
   1. Caterpillars--Juvenile literature. I. Title. II. Series.

QL544.2.C43 2006
595.78'139--dc22

                                        2005012450

Acknowledgments
The publishers would like to thank the following for permission to reproduce photographs: Alamy Images pp. 8 (Daniel L Geiger/SNAP), 10 (Papilo/Pobert Pickett), 14; Corbis pp. 12 (Ron Sanford), 20 (Gary W Carter); Oxford Scientific Films pp. 4, 5, 6, 7, 9 (Animals Animals/Carroll W Perkins), 11, 13 (Brian Kenney), 15, 16, 17, 18, 19, 21 (Animals Animal/Patti Murray), 22, 23 top, 23 bottom (Animals Animals.)

Cover picture of a caterpillar reproduced with permission of Nature Picture Library.

Every effort has been made to contact copyright holders of any material reproduced in this book. Any omissions will be rectified in subsequent printings if notice is given to the publishers.

Some words are shown in bold, **like this**. You can find out what they mean by looking in the glossary on page 24.

Contents

Caterpillars

Caterpillars are small creatures.

5

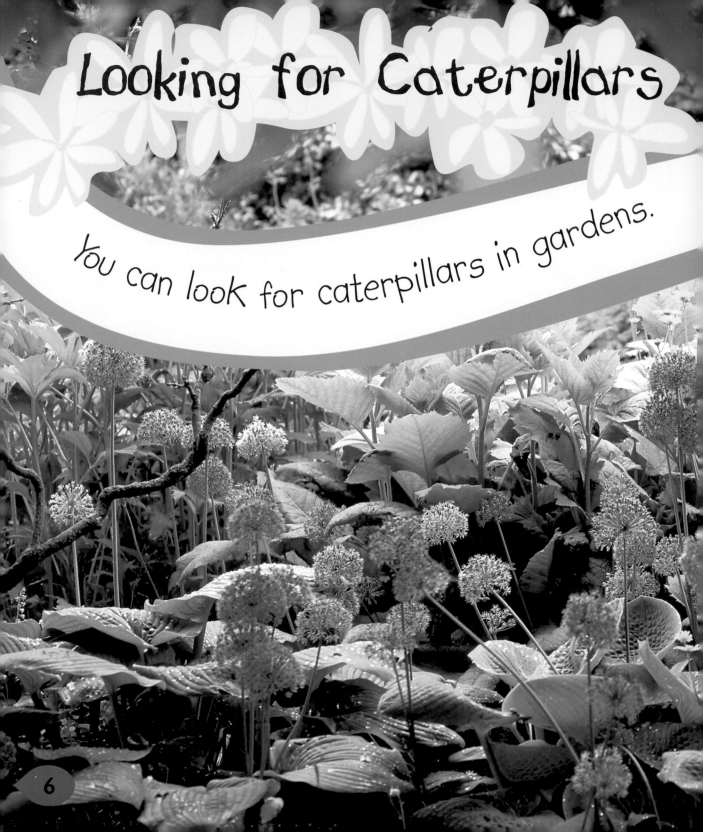

Looking for Caterpillars

You can look for caterpillars in gardens.

You might find caterpillars
on leaves in the summer.

A Caterpillar's Body

Caterpillars have soft bodies.
They can be **hairy** or **spiky**.

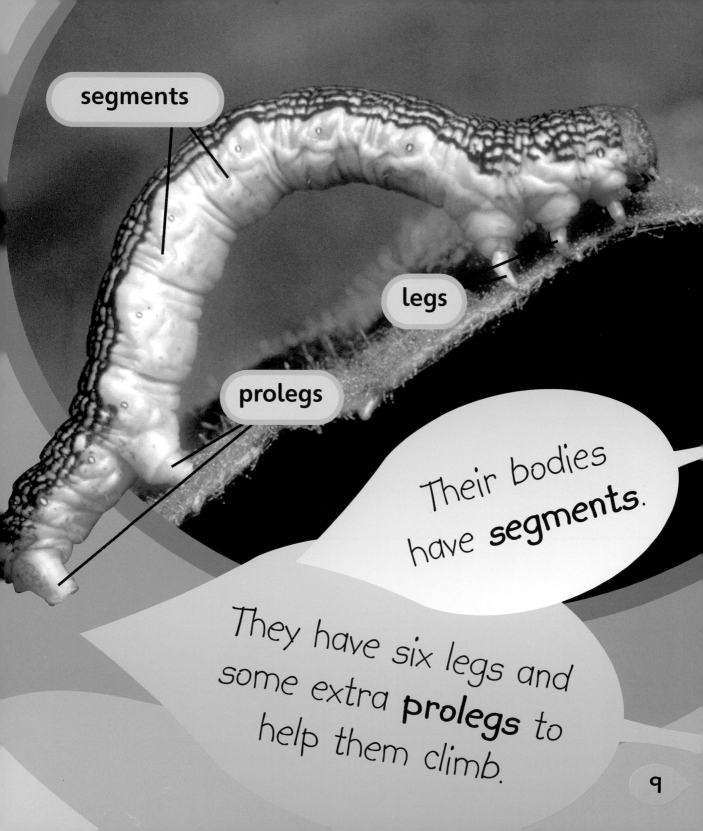

Young Caterpillars

A female butterfly lays a tiny egg on a leaf.

After a few days a caterpillar **hatches** out of the egg.

Food for Caterpillars

Young caterpillars are always hungry.

They **munch** their way through leaves very quickly!

Growing Up

The caterpillar eats and eats and eats. It gets bigger and **bigger** and **bigger!**

A caterpillar grows so fast that it has to shed its skin.

From Caterpillar to Chrysalis

When a caterpillar has grown as **big** as it can, it hangs from a twig.

The caterpillar turns its skin into a hard **chrysalis**.

From Chrysalis to Butterfly

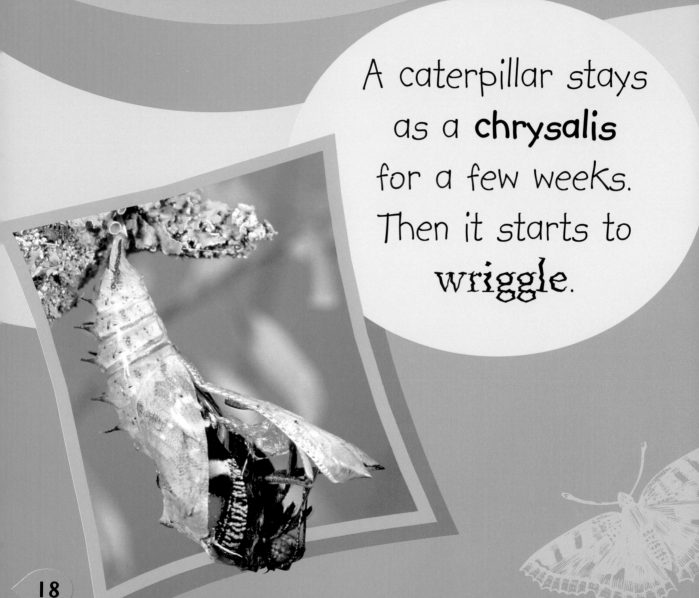

A caterpillar stays as a **chrysalis** for a few weeks. Then it starts to **wriggle**.

The chrysalis opens. The caterpillar has turned into a butterfly!

Caterpillars in Danger

Birds, wasps, and mice all like to eat caterpillars.

Some caterpillars are **poisonous**. Some use **spikes** to **protect** themselves.

21

Types of Caterpillars

There are thousands of different kinds of caterpillars.

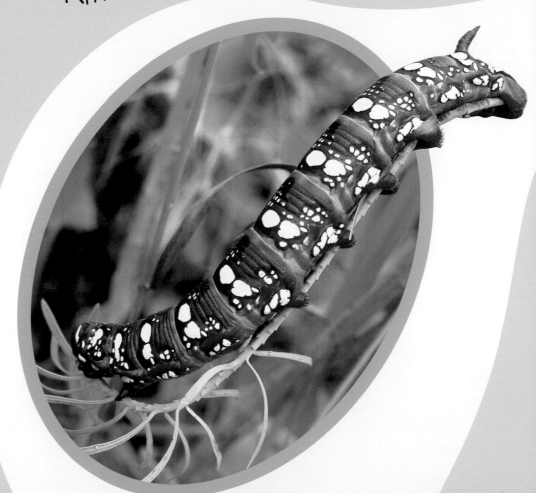

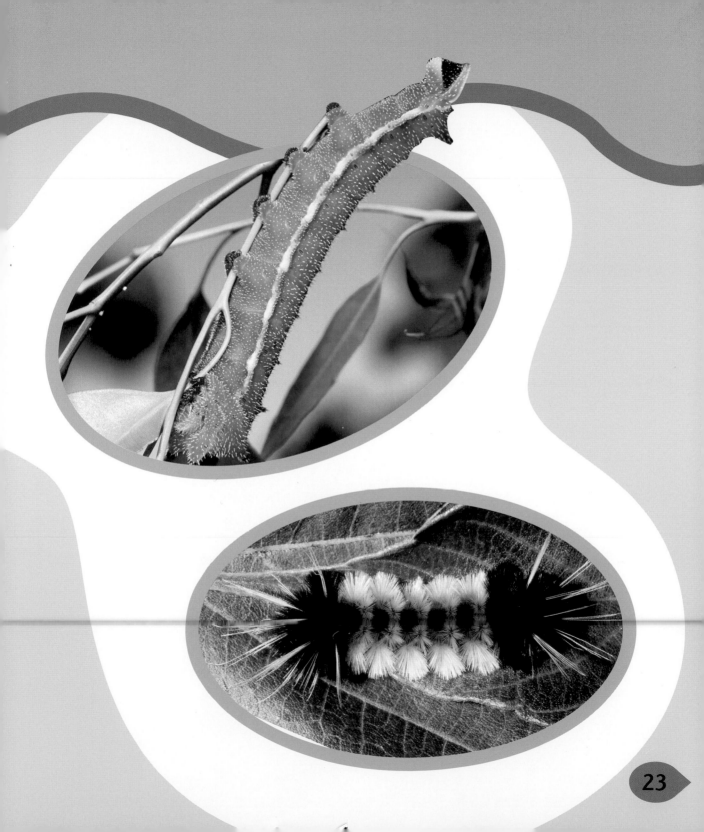

Glossary

chrysalis caterpillar turning into a butterfly

hatch to come out of an egg

poisonous dangerous to eat or touch

prolegs legs that disappear when a caterpillar becomes a butterfly

protect keep safe

segments small sections that make up a caterpillar's body

Index

Notes for Adults

This series supports the young child's exploration of their learning environment and their knowledge and understanding of their world. Using the books in the series together will enable comparisons of similarities and differences to be made. (NB. Many of the photographs in **Creepy Creatures** show them much larger than life size. The first spread of each title shows the creature at approximately its real life size.)

These books will help the child extend their vocabulary, as they will hear new words. Some of the words that may be new to them in **Caterpillars** are *chrysalis*, *poisonous*, and *hatches*. Since words are used in context in the book this should enable the young child to gradually incorporate them into their own vocabulary.

Additional Information

Butterflies can "taste" plants with their legs to choose where to lay their eggs. This means that their caterpillars will hatch straight onto the best leaves for them to eat. Lots of caterpillars eat their eggshell once they have hatched as it contains valuable nutrients. Caterpillars have 3 pairs of "true legs," like other insects, and up to 5 pairs of "prolegs" that are suckers for gripping leaves. Some caterpillars use their coloring to blend in with their surroundings. Others are brightly colored to warn predators that they are poisonous. Caterpillars are found all over the world and there are thousands of different varieties.

Follow-up Activities

The child can record what they have found out about caterpillars—especially their life cycle—by drawing, painting, and writing. Also relate factual information to stories such as *The Very Hungry Caterpillar* by Eric Carle.